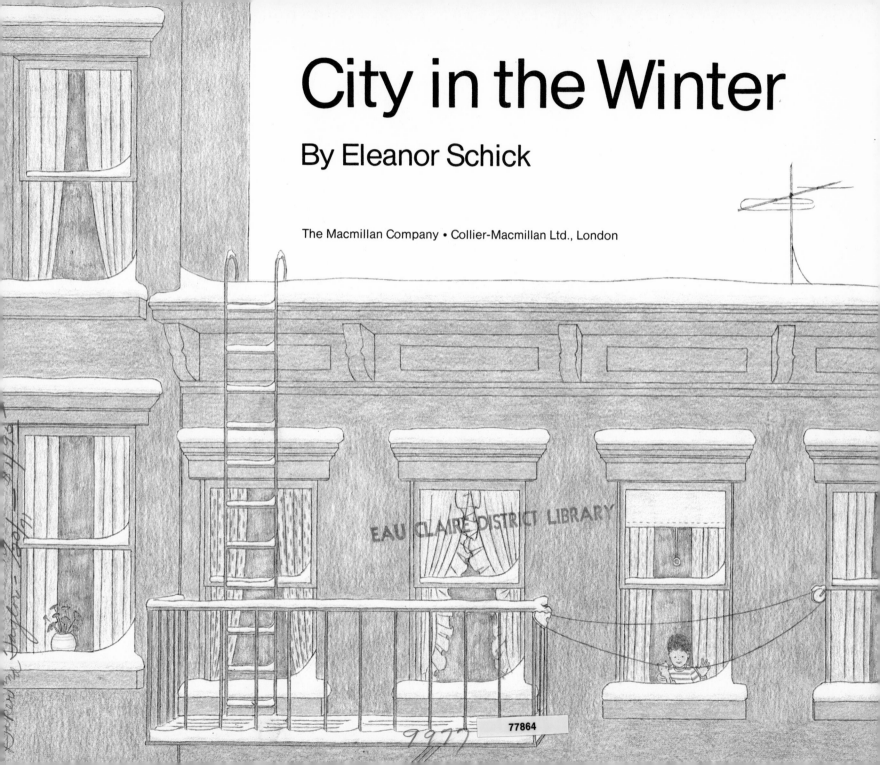

City in the Winter

By Eleanor Schick

The Macmillan Company • Collier-Macmillan Ltd., London

For Jack with love

It was early morning.

The radiators had begun to clank and sputter.

Outside it was snowing.

It was warm in Jimmy's bed,

but soon he would have to dress for school.

In the kitchen Grandma was preparing breakfast.
Jimmy's mother was getting ready to go to work. There
was music on the radio. Then someone interrupted to say
the schools were closed because of the blizzard.
"What's a blizzard?" asked Jimmy.

"Look out the window," said his mother.
And then he saw.
There was snow everywhere.
It was falling fast, in big white flakes
and blowing around and around in circles.

"You and Grandma will have a good time today," said Jimmy's mother, "but there's no snow holiday for me." She put on her warmest coat and scarf. "I'll have to hurry because the buses will be slow," she said. Then she kissed Jimmy and left to go to work.

It was strange not to be going to school.
Jimmy listened to his mother's boots
clopping in the hall. And then Grandma
called him to the table for breakfast.

The kettle was puffing on the stove. Outside, the snow was blowing hard against the window pane. Jimmy wondered about the cats who lived in the yard next door. He pretended they were in the kitchen with him, eating hot breakfasts and staying warm beside the radiator.

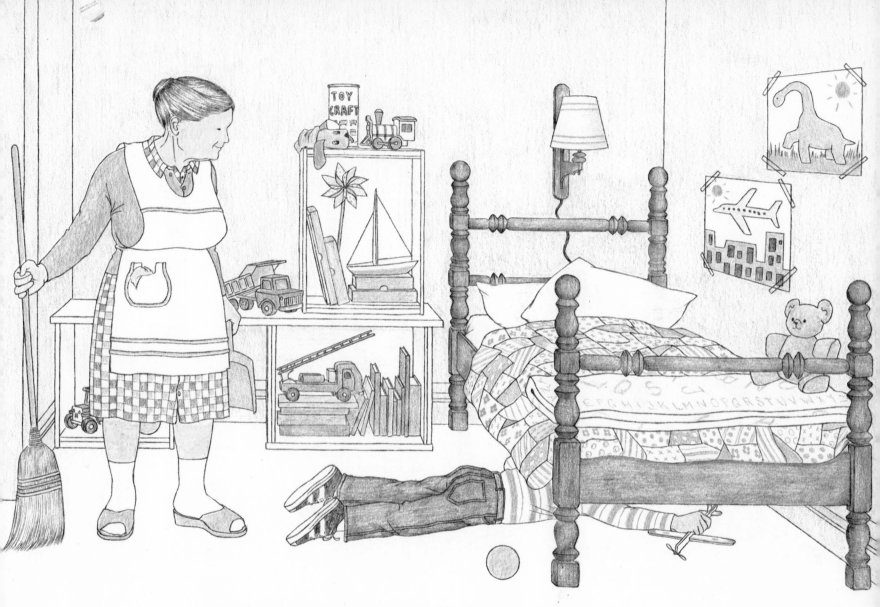

After breakfast Grandma made the beds.
Jimmy helped to fold the blankets,
and held the dustpan while Grandma swept.
"Here's my lost airplane!" he said.

Grandma said it was one of those days that are
good for doing things you never get around to doing.
So she took out her sewing and sat down.
Jimmy couldn't think of anything to do.

Grandma found a cardboard box and showed him
how to cut out windows and a door. When he
finished, he crayoned it red. "It's a barn," Jimmy said.
"My animals are snowed in just like we are."

Soon it was twelve o'clock. Grandma got the lunch box
she had packed the night before. "It looks like a picnic,"
Jimmy said. "I'm going to eat on the floor."

But the floor was cold, so he sat on pillows, and Grandma made
hot chocolate. "I've never had a winter picnic before," said Jimmy.
And he took his animals out of the barn so they could watch.

When lunch was finished Grandma said, "Let's make a
garden." So she and Jimmy planted a sweet potato.
Jimmy stuck the toothpicks in carefully, and filled the jar
with water. He wished it would hurry up and grow.

Jimmy wandered over to the window. The snow had stopped, and the sun was out. On the roof next door some sparrows were fighting for a tiny piece of food.

Jimmy asked Grandma for some bread
and he threw it down in little pieces
so each bird could have some for himself.
But they saw him and flew away.

In a few minutes he looked again and saw, not birds,
but tiny footprints in the snow where the bread had been.

Grandma said that they could go out and buy some milk.

She knew that Jimmy wanted to go down to see the snow.

It was much colder than Jimmy thought it would be. He could

hardly move his arms because he had so many sweaters on.

Everywhere the snow was deep.

They couldn't even see the sidewalks.

So Jimmy walked behind Grandma, stepping

in her boot prints and holding on to her coat.

There were no cars or trucks moving.
There was no sound except the wind blowing
and the crunch of footsteps, and far away
the scraping noise of someone shoveling snow.

Finally they got to the store, and the door was locked.

"We have just enough milk for tonight," said Grandma.

"Let's go home and get warm!"

It was good to be inside again.
They climbed the stairs and the
snow melted off their boots.

Jimmy's hands began to sting as they got warmer.
He could smell the dinners cooking in other people's
apartments. It made him hungry.

When they got upstairs they took off their
snowy clothes and went into the kitchen.
"What we need is some good hot soup,"
said Grandma.

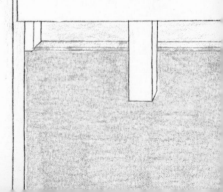

Jimmy peeled the onions and washed the vegetables.
When he set the table he put his garden in the middle
for his mother to see when she got home.

Then he lined up his animals on the windowsill to watch the sun go down. He waited as the sky turned orange, then purple, and then dark. Grandma waited too.

But it was a long time before they heard the sound of boots
stamping in the hall and the key turning in the lock.
Jimmy ran to the door to hug his mother.
"I'm so glad you're home from the blizzard," he shouted.

At dinner Jimmy told his mother how
he had made the barn and the garden.

And before he went to bed he pointed out the window to the
footprints in the snow. But it was much too dark to see them.
"You can show them to me in the morning, before you go to
school," his mother said.

And she kissed him goodnight, and he went to sleep.